Saint Jude's Kitchen

Johannes T. Evans

After an injury stops him working, a failing deckhand gets a new lease on life.

20k, rated M, cis M/M romance and light comedy! Themes around cooking and nurturing, identity and sense of self, and complex family dynamics.

Content warnings for emotional abuse and implied physical abuse, some racial microaggressions, severe social anxiety, self-esteem issues. There's food kink and feeding kink throughout, with weight gain referenced as a part of that, but the tone is more about food as a manifestation of nurturing and love rather than being about weight gain or feeding itself as a fetish.

Saint Jude's Kitchen is a work of fiction created from the author's imagination. Any resemblance to living persons, living or dead, or resemblance to actual events, places, or names is purely coincidental.

Cover design by Johannes T. Evans.

Saint Jude's Kitchen

It was Jude's ninth day in a row drinking in the Marlin.

His leg hurt, naturally, and it was going to *naturally* hurt for fucking months. There was a half-completed sudoku open on the page in front of him, but whatever fucking internet article said that sudokus were good if you were bored and had a broken leg was full of fucking shit. He'd gone through a third of the book so far, and he was pretty sure he'd filled out a lot of them wrong.

He was no good at sudokus, it turned out.

The Marlin was a Scottish-owned pub, but he wasn't the only American in it, at least — he liked Philipsburg, most of the time, but he normally liked it when he had two working legs and he was mostly drinking and partying. They had the house here, sure, but Saint Martin wasn't really *home*, not like Long Island was home.

He'd wanted to book a flight home once they finally let him out of the hospital, but his dad had nixed the idea, and he'd gotten tired of staying at home within a day — it wasn't the hospital, but it wasn't much better. It was not even that he liked people, necessarily — he didn't talk to anyone, was uncomfortable when people came up to him and tried to make small talk about his fucking leg, but he liked that there *were* people, liked that they were there.

He didn't like to be on his own. He wasn't used to it, didn't think he ever would be.

He'd been on his own a lot, in the hospital.

People had visited, a little. One or two friends had dropped in, yachties between charters, anyone who was on the island, but none of them were people he normally saw sober, and it felt weird, having them come in to see him when he was hopped up on morphine and couldn't concentrate on fucking anything, when he was irritable and looked like shit, too.

He was thirty-two years old.

Thirty-two years old, with a broken leg, and no friends — and he'd broken his leg because he was a shit deckhand, and he was shit at sudoku, too, was a little shit at basically everything.

His dad had started on him about applying to work on other boats again, to work towards his captain's license, to do basically anything other than what he was doing — and now, he couldn't even try, because he was going to be in a cast for months, *plus* the PT, and in the meantime, he couldn't even sail.

"You've been here all day again," was the crisp remark from some fuck he couldn't remember the name of, and Jude looked up at him. He was the Philipsburg harbourmaster, had been for several years — they'd been in school together — and he was a tall, speccy fuck who needed glasses to see.

"Didn't know I needed your permission," he drawled. "What, I need to fill in some bullshit form just for this?"

"You might do something useful for once."

Jude scoffed, sipping his beer, and the harbourmaster sat down in the chair beside him, making him stare.

He knew this guy, knew he was a dick, that he was always riding his dad's ass, riding everyone's ass, too regimented and stuck on the wrong shit.

"The fuck are you doing?" he demanded.

"Reading my book," was the harbourmaster's blunt reply, "and drinking my wine. The pub is full, and as you have no friends likely to join you, my harbour blesseadly empty of your extended family, so I thought I'd commandeer half of your table. Problem?"

"I'm not a fucking *poof* like you are, you know," he said, and the harbourmaster arched an eyebrow at him. Jude mimicked the harbourmaster's mostly-British accent to put the emphasis on the word, hoping it would be enough to put him off, but he didn't seem deterred.

"Aren't you?" he asked softly. "Oh, no. Imagine my shock and surprise." He said it in a deadpan way, cool and cutting (British or Dutch, his accent was kind of made for it), and then looked down at the text of his book. "I'm not interested in you anyway."

That stung, for some reason, and before Jude could consider why he even cared, he was asking, "Why not?"

"I like men who know what they want from life, that's all."

"I fucking — What does that even *mean*?"

"It means you don't cut the mustard. I wouldn't take it personally — there's a rare sailor who does."

Jude wasn't as drunk as he'd like to be. He'd been buzzed all day, but not actually drunk, and now he stared at the harbourmaster, took in his neat clothes and his e-reader and... *him*.

"You ever even *been* on a boat?" he demanded.

The quartermaster gave a short, sharp laugh. "I grew up on a fishing trawler," he said. Looking up from his book now, he made eye contact, staring Jude down. "Unlike some people I could mention, I have experience on real sea vessels, and not merely fancy little yachts for hire by the rich. Have *you* ever been on a fishing vessel, hm? A merchant trading vessel, even?"

Jude set his jaw and didn't say anything.

"Mmm, precisely," said the harbourmaster. "Just catamarans and yachts. I like very much to be at sea — I like even more to do my duty ensuring that other sailors have a safe port to return to. That you don't respect that is irrelevant."

"I didn't say that," said Jude irritably. "But you shouldn't be surprised people hate you when you spend your days riding everyone's dick about shit that doesn't matter."

"With competent sailors, I don't need to."

"You're fucking lucky I can't get up right now."

The harbourmaster laughed. It was a smug, superior sound, and he condescendingly patted Jude's hand, which he immediately wrenched away. "Bless your heart, thinking you could fight a man like me. That really is sweet, in its way."

Jude was pissed, his hands clenching into fists, and the harbourmaster turned to look at him over his glasses. His eyes were an uncomfortable blue, a pale colour that was almost silver — Jude didn't know what he was, exactly, but he wasn't white Dutch or British, and even though his skin wasn't *super* dark, it was the darkest skin he'd ever seen against eyes that pale.

"Your father," said the harbourmaster softly, "is a bully and a fool. You're better than him."

"Fuck you," spat Jude. "You don't know a fucking thing about my father."

"If that's the case, then we have it in common," was the harbourmaster's infuriatingly smooth reply, and he didn't say anything more, looking back to his book and sipping at his wine.

Jude sat in furious silence.

He kept taking the seat beside him, as the week passed by. So long as Jude was there after the end of the day, which he normally still was, the harbourmaster would settle down in the empty seat like they were friends, like it was normal, often without saying a thing, and when he did say something, it was fucking annoying.

"Are you going to sit here every day for the entirety of your recovery?" he asked mildly one evening.

"The fuck else am I meant to do? I can't exactly join a crew on one leg."

"I really don't know. Take a course in something, go to the library, watch a film, take up fishing, knitting, chess... You know, something other than sitting here and miserably drinking beer as you fail to fill in a sudoku."

Jude stared at him balefully, and drank some of his beer.

"Mm, I thought so," said the harbourmaster, marking his page with a fancy little magnetic bookmark and getting to his feet. He swapped between dull-looking paperbacks and shit on his e-reader. It was a little after half-nine, and he usually left around this time, only sticking around for an hour or two. "Want a ride home?"

"What?"

"I drive. Sam," he nodded to the bartender, "says you've been getting taxis. Do you want a ride home?"

"I'm not going to suck your fucking cock," said Jude.

The harbourmaster, nonplussed, said, "I don't recall offering to let you. To be clear, my offer is to drive you to where you live, pour you onto your yard path, and then drive on. With respect, I take rather good care of my cock, and I only trust it to those who'd know what to do with it."

Jude stared at him, and the harbourmaster drained the last of the juice in his glass — he always drank one small glass of wine and something else after, was probably obsessed with his blood alcohol volume — and set both his glass and Jude's empty beer bottle on the bar.

"Fine," said Jude. "Thanks, I guess."

"You guess," snorted the harbourmaster.

He had a little eco-friendly car, and Jude bit back anything he could say about it although a lot came to mind, moving forward on his crutches. The harbourmaster opened the door for him, taking his crutches from him once he was sat in the passenger side and laying them on the back seat."

The car wasn't as fancy as he thought from the outside. He'd assumed the harbourmaster would drive an automatic like a lot of the Europeans did, but the car had a stick shift. He didn't have a radio, just an empty slot where he had a pocket-sized dressing kit and just enough space to shove his phone in beside it, and apart from the air freshener, he had some stickers on the dash and some nerdy painted figurines, goblins or some shit. It was extremely clean, with little hanging storage baskets hung on the backs of the seats, and on the passenger side there was a first aid kit and spare lifejackets — his trunk was probably full of even more stuff like that.

"You grew up on a trawler?" asked Jude as the harbourmaster sank into the driver's seat.

"I did," he said, putting his hand on the back of Jude's seat as he looked behind, pulling out from the narrow gap he'd parked in — but with a dinky little car like this, Jude supposed parallel parking was a lot fucking easier. "Rough seas, hard work."

"What, you think what yachties do isn't hard work?" demanded Jude, and the harbourmaster laughed. Once he was out on the road, his hands on the wheel were at a perfect ten and two.

"All sailing is hard work," he said mildly. "You want me to disparage your private charters to justify *your* disrespect of fishermen, merchants, and rig workers. Sorry to disappoint you, but it's not appealing bait."

"Why'd you hate me then?"

He laughed again.

"I don't *hate* you, you idiot," he said dryly. "I've been drinking with you all week and am currently driving you home. Do you do that with your enemies?"

"You hate my dad."

"I hate bad sailors. They make my job harder."

"The fuck is your job anyway?" asked Jude, rolling his eyes. "You're a glorified traffic controller. Taking people's licenses down for the insurance guys, trying to interfere with the right of way—"

"Right of way," repeated the harbourmaster, again with a little laugh. "As if you'd know the first thing about it."

"Obsessed with safety protocol and shit."

"You know, I am," was his even-toned reply. "I don't much like to see sailors or passengers injured or dead — your leg is broken because your yacht wasn't properly tethered, your passerelle wasn't solidly deployed, and you never wear proper shoes to work in."

"Fuck *off*, my leg is broken because I fucking slipped carrying a—"

"Shut your mouth a moment," the harbourmaster interrupted him. "Had your lines been taut, you wouldn't have been moving so much in the water, and your yacht wouldn't have been veering so close to the ship beside you. Had you been wearing shoes with a proper grip on them, you might not have been so unsteady on your feet. And *crucially*, had your passerelle been properly deployed and fastened in the first place, you almost certainly wouldn't have been as injured as you were. I saw that fall from start to finish: I saw you slip, I saw the box tip forward. You twisted right, you fell *almost* into the water, with your leg keeping you up — and as if in slow motion, I saw the box hit the third segment of your gangway, saw the whole thing suddenly extend fully, and I could see your leg *crunch* before I heard you fucking scream. All of this before your idiot brothers were dragging you out of the water with no support on your back *or* your leg, twisting your leg further in the process. Given that I've watched you carry things incorrectly all our lives, it's a miracle you didn't slip discs in your back as *well* as fuck your leg up, but carrying the box was the *least* of the problems there."

Jude had never heard him curse before, let alone got a lecture like that from him, but before he could comment on it, the harbourmaster pulled up onto their drive. He got out to open the car door for him, handing him his crutches.

"You want help with the front door?"

"Nah," said Jude, rolling his eyes again. "I think I'm fine without Mr Health and fucking Safety looking over my shoulder."

The harbourmaster hummed an amused sound, and plucked a piece of lint off his collar. His hand was warm. "I suppose you can call me Rich if you like. No need for the *Mr*."

Jude didn't know what the fuck to make of that, but Rich was already getting back into his car.

"See you tomorrow," he called pleasantly, and drove off.

Maria had been in and cleaned while Jude was out, and had left a plate covered over for him, some kind of Mexican rice thing. It made Jude smile when he peeled back the plate and saw it — she almost never cooked stuff like this when his dad was around, and he ate on his feet, leaning on the counter, before he rinsed the plate off and tossed it in the dishwasher.

He was sleeping in the guest bedroom for the time being, just 'cause it was on the ground floor and he didn't have to fuck around with the stairs, plus it had an en suite.

He grunted as he fell down onto the bed, his whole leg aching, and he turned on his good side, shoving his face into the pillow.

He remembered the clank the passerelle had made as it had fully telescoped out, hadn't even realised it wasn't solid until he'd *felt* it.

It took him ages to get to sleep.

* * *

"Do you really think I'm a bad sailor?" he asked the next evening.

"You're a terrible deckhand," said Rich. "I've seen you on those little pocket cruisers, and you're fine on those — I assume you're not terrible on a catamaran. But you don't have any business handling a thing on a bigger vessel, let alone a yacht like the Island Time. I think you have discipline, but it's misdirected — your father's vessels are always very clean, but *not* always safely moored. You've been trained to rank appearance over safety, and the only reason you get away with it is because smaller vessels rush out of the way because *they* won't get the worst damage."

"Appearance *is* important," said Jude. "What, you think we should look like the fucking rustbuckets that always roll in and out, paintjobs all over the place? No fucking uniforms, no class?"

"A neatly pressed uniform isn't going to save a man's life. An improperly tied line could take one, however. Those *rustbuckets* you so despise take safety seriously — they go out on rougher seas for longer hours. It's life or death out there, and they catch the fish you serve to your guests, I might point out."

Jude scoffed, and Rich laid his chin on his hand, looking at him seriously. "Do you *want* to be a sailor?"

"I *am* a sailor."

"Rankless," he replied, "at thirty-something. A deckhand, not even a boatswain. You've not even tried for your captain's license — what do you have, your basic STCW certs, crowd management training, a basic first aider's cert that you don't feel confident using?"

"Coming from the man who's got half the port clinic packed in the back of his car."

"And knows how to use it," said Rich, and Jude shivered, rolling his shoulders, not knowing why the fuck him saying that made him feel small and shitty and... weird.

"What more am I meant to want?"

"Satisfaction. A job you like, a job that satisfies you — work that satisfies you. Work you're proud of."

"I'm proud."

"Of your father," said Rich, clucking his tongue. "Not the labour he gives you."

"Fuck you."

"Ha. If you earn it, maybe."

Jude looked warily at Rich, wasn't sure what to make of that, but Rich didn't flinch, just kept his gaze.

"I'm not gay," said Jude.

"Alright," said Rich.

"And if I *was* gay, I'd be fucking hunks. Not four-eyed dicks like you."

"I'm already *so* out of your league," said Rich, laughing and shaking his bed. "You really think you could do better than me?"

Rich *was* hot. He was young for a harbourmaster, and he was tall, strong, had thick, glossy black hair, a nice moustache and goatee, and his skin was warm brown with a few freckles and moles. His eyes were light in colour, yeah, but his eyelashes were thick and dark.

Jude wasn't bad-looking. He had a strong jaw, good cheekbones. His hair was nice, he thought. He wasn't the kind of guy that girls turned to look at like Rich, but then, Rich was fucking gay, so what was the point in him looking that good to girls anyway?

"If you're so out of my league, why the fuck do you hang out with me?"

"Your name is Jude, isn't it?" asked Rich. "Perhaps I've an unhealthy attraction to hopeless cases."

Jude looked at him, and said, "Haven't you got actual friends?"

Rich smiled thinly. "I suppose I'm not good at making them."

"Did you go to college?"

"No. Couldn't afford it."

"That why you're so bitter?"

Rich laughed. "What am I missing out on? Going to college like you did and failing out of two different degrees?"

"How do *you* know that?"

"I'm harbourmaster, don't you know," said Rich in an easy purr. "People tell me almost everything."

Jude sat back in his chair, wrinkling his nose because the wind was cool today, and it made his leg ache in its cast.

"You still have your parents?" asked Jude.

"My mother died at sea. Lost during a storm. My father lost his arm in an accident on a trawler when I was twenty, and he retired — he lives up on the French side. I drive up and visit on my days off."

Jude looked at him cautiously, and asked, "How'd he lose his arm?"

"They'd been blown off course by a squall, and they were too far into shallower waters for comfort. They laid anchor before they could be thrown off further, into the real shallows, or even run aground. There was some sort of malfunction with the mechanism, winds roaring, rain falling, and they were in a hurry — he tried to loosen it, and it did come loose, but all of a sudden. Chain won against flesh and bone, I'm afraid."

"What does he do now?"

"He makes sails," said Rich. "You can take him off the water, but you can't take the sail out of his hands."

"Hand," said Jude, and he didn't know why he said it, expected to be yelled at, but Rich laughed.

"Yeah," he murmured.

"You close with him?"

"My father? No, not really. He's quite a hard man. He loves me, I love him, but we struggle with one another. We're different men, both of us very stubborn, set in our positions — we provoke one another, whether we mean to or not. It's easier for us to love one another with so much distance between us."

"You shouldn't disrespect your father," said Jude, and Rich tilted his head, peering at him with interest.

"You think that I don't respect him?"

"It shouldn't matter whether you agree. He's your dad — you shouldn't contradict him."

"My father taught me to contradict him," said Rich simply.

Jude couldn't tell if that was a joke or not, couldn't tell how it was intended or how he was meant to reply, if he was meant to reply at all.

After he'd been silent for a few seconds, Rich chuckled, and said, "Checkmate!" before he waved over the bartender.

* * *

His father said, when they came back for a day between charters, "People say you've been hanging around with that homo harbourmaster."

"Not really," said Jude. "He just hangs around me."

"Probably trying to fuck you," said Jonah.

"Probably is," agreed his father.

Jude shrugged, staring down at the table, and waited for the subject to change. He weathered it until it did.

He wondered how he'd answer if any of them asked what else he'd been doing at home when he couldn't sail, but no one did.

* * *

"What jobs are meant to satisfy me?" asked Jude when his dad had set sail again, and Rich looked at him across the table. He always brought his book, but he didn't normally open it anymore, just set it aside and concentrated on Jude.

It was weird, having his full attention, just the two of them sitting down together. Jude normally sat with his back against the wall, to the side of the table, but Rich faced the table, and that also meant facing Jude — he didn't think he'd ever sat down with *anybody* like this, before now, sat down with just one person across a small table. It was too intimate, too direct.

James was older than he was, and Jonah was two years younger, but they were always together, the three of them, so he'd never even really been one-on-one with his mom or dad.

It wasn't—

Bad.

"Is that a set-up for a double entendre?" asked Rich, and Jude frowned at him.

"What? Jesus, no."

"Alright."

"I meant... There's nothing else here."

"Take classes."

"What in?"

"Am I meant to decide for you?"

When Rich excused himself to piss, he went out to his car before he came back inside, and he tossed him a catalogue for local day classes.

It was all either shit he already knew how to do — how to sail, how to surf, how to tie knots — or shit for middle-aged women like life drawing, cooking, photography, *flower* arrangements.

He said this out loud to Rich, and Rich didn't laugh.

"Don't you like women?" he asked.

"Yeah, sure, I like women," said Jude. "Doesn't mean I want to fucking be one."

"Presumably you like to meet them, though. If you think these classes will be replete with single women, that's ideal for you, no? What the fuck is your damage?"

Jude swallowed, because something about Rich cursing into his face, all dry and calm, made him hot in a way he didn't want to think about, in a way he *refused* to think about, and he leaned back in his seat.

"Gardening," said Rich, looking at the page. "Is earth and flowers going to be such a threat to your delicate manhood?"

"No, it's gross," said Jude. "Dirt. Mud. I like sand — you can trust sand. It washes off. Dirt *sticks*."

"No dirt," repeated Rich. "Woodcraft?"

"The fuck is that?"

"Wooden sculptures, I think. Carpentry on a small scale."

"Sounds like bullshit," muttered Jude.

"... If you say so. Photography?"

"I don't need a class to take photos. I have a smartphone."

"Cooking, then."

"Who the fuck am I going to cook for?"

"You don't eat?"

Jude pulled the catalogue toward him and looked at the page. "It's five days a week," he said. "All day."

"For six weeks — it's an intensive course, but it should keep you busy, and with all the beer you drink, I expect it'll even be cheaper. I know their pottery teacher uses a wheelchair, so I'm sure they can accommodate your crutches, or have something for you to sit on."

"Like the old people, you mean?" asked Jude bitterly.

"If you want to hop around your little kitchen block one-legged, I'm sure that can be accommodated," said Rich dryly. "There aren't any rules against embarrassing yourself if that's your passion."

"You're such an asshole."

"I do my best."

"Fine," said Jude. "I'll take a cooking class, and next, I'll take a class in sucking dick. Will that make you happy?"

"Oh, it will delight me, yes," said Rich. "It's so nice for a man to be educated."

Jude sniggered without meaning to, and Rich smiled.

Jude signed up for the class.

* * *

He didn't know anything about cooking. His mother used to cook at home, and after they'd broken up, his dad paid the housekeeper extra to do it. Maria was a good cook too, but Jude always told her not to bother cooking for him most of the time — he mostly ordered in, or ate stuff that didn't need cooking.

When they were home in Long Island, they ate out all the time, and his mom worked too many hours to have time for cooking most of the time now.

The class started with how to boil an egg.

It was a relief.

He was nervous about the burners, about how hot they were, but it was surprisingly easy to just drop the egg in the water, leave it to the timer. They ate their eggs while watching the tutor, a woman with brawny arms, show them different knives and how to use them.

There were women in the class — most of them were young women in their twenties, and then there were older guys, guys in their forties, fifties, one guy in his sixties. It was mostly tourists and people out here for the season, but the old guy was a local, and he asked how Jude's leg was healing up, and Jude told him it was fine.

The actual cooking, though, it was... interesting.

More interesting than he expected.

The tutor talked about how food came together, not just how to cook it, prepare it, but she talked about chemical reactions in food, how things changed when they were heated, how that affected taste, texture.

It wasn't just about heating it so you didn't get sick, it turned out.

Most foods had compounds in them that were *volatile* — which didn't mean explosive, apparently, just that they could be evaporated or broken down easily. When you heated something up, those compounds could break up and permeate the rest of the dish, and that made them more flavourful, and they emitted stronger smells, too. You didn't just taste food by *tasting* it, you smelled it, too, and that made odour important.

And your tastebuds couldn't take food that was too hot, but humans were hot-blooded, and your tastebuds were calibrated for heat — when you ate cold food, chilling your tastebuds could numb them a little, because you had less blood flow to the area.

He supposed he knew some of it, but it never really sunk in like that, never connected altogether or applied to food and eating and cooking. It was cool, seeing the syllabus, what they were going to go over — there was even one day where they'd look at some cocktails and wine pairings, talk about different beers.

"How was it?" asked Rich when he came to sit down in the Marlin.

Jude didn't want to sound stupid, saying he was excited about how food tasted different when you heated it up, and he was pretty sure that *would* sound stupid.

"It was fine," said Jude.

Rich smiled. "Good."

* * *

The first week they concentrated on staples.

Eggs: boiling eggs, scrambling eggs, poaching eggs, omelettes, French toast. Potatoes: mashed potatoes, baked potatoes and potato skins, fries, gratin (you pre-cooked the potatoes) and dauphinoise (you put the potatoes in raw). They looked at different kinds of rice, how you cooked them.

The whole time, they talked about the ways different proteins reacted to heat and moisture, how the presence of different starches affected texture and taste, the difference between the effects of high heat or lower heat for longer, and heat from all angles in the oven or the microwave versus heat from a pan or a grill.

The first Friday, they made fresh pasta, and Jude lost himself in kneading the dough and passing it through the machine to flatten it out. He couldn't decide on just one sort of pasta, wanted to try all the kinds he could — he made a bow, a shell, made little twists, couldn't quite get the hang of the spirals.

He wanted to learn their names. He wanted to learn how to do them all, wanted to make the ones he was trying to make look perfect — and he wanted to make stuffed pastas, too, because they weren't doing that today, but it looked *cool*.

It tasted good, the pasta, even without any sauce on it, but Vanessa showed them a simple cream sauce at the end of the day. The container of pasta was still warm in his satchel when he went into the Marlin, and he immediately took it out and pushed it across to Rich.

He looked surprised, but he took the fork handed to him, opened the container, speared a few mismatched fresh pasta shapes, and took a bite.

Jude stared at Rich's face as he let out a low, pleased hum, his eyes closing shut, and he drew the fork out from between closed lips. His eyelashes fluttered slightly, and Jude's mouth felt dry.

"That's fucking *good*," he said lowly, pulling the container closer to him. "What's in this?"

"The pasta's fresh, um, just egg and flour. And the sauce is cream, garlic, uh, parmesan, another Italian cheese I don't remember, spinach — you like it?"

"I certainly do," said Rich. "I hope you weren't expecting me to give this back."

"Nah," said Jude, feeling suddenly hot for no reason as he sank into his chair, put his crutches aside, reached for the beer Rich had waiting for him. "Haven't eaten today?"

"Not anything this good," said Rich. "You really don't mind?"

"No, no, I've been eating all day," Jude said hurriedly. He wondered if Rich would comment on it, the fact that Jude just sat there and watched him eat, watched the shift of Rich's jaw as he chewed.

He kept letting out blissful noises, and it was—

Yeah. Maybe it was hot, but it'd be hot if a girl was enjoying something he'd made this much too.

"Does everyone — know this stuff?" he asked, and Rich glanced up at him.

"Know what?"

"About the proteins in pasta dough," said Jude, and Rich blinked at him uncertainly, and the relief he felt was so strong that it almost distracted him from the heat between his legs. "So, so there's protein in flour, right? Gliadin and, and glutenin, and when they're combined, they make gluten, which is what makes that slightly sweet thickness that you taste? And when you knead them, it warms up those strands, and then they expand and you bond together the molecules. And when people say dough has a good structure, that means that there's this whole gluten *network* — so then when it's heated up, like, for bread, that means yeast is spread out so it proofs and bakes the same all over, and there's little bubbles of gas from the baking soda or the yeast, that's what makes the bubbles in the white of the bread, but... But for pasta, you know, you need that structure so that once you start rolling it, the gluten strands are robust enough to survive it, and the pasta dough stays slightly springy, and then you have that slight chewy texture, you know? So it's not just... mushy?"

He'd blurted it out all at once, was almost out of breath, and he felt his cheeks burn red with embarrassment, so he hurried to drink some of his beer. Rich was staring at him, his eyes slightly wide, so that the light colour of his eyes looked even lighter.

"Sorry," he said.

"Don't be sorry," said Rich. "You're smiling — I don't think I've seen you smile since before you broke that leg. Did you enjoy it?" The container was empty of pasta, and he was licking the fork clean.

"Well," said Jude. "I don't think making pasta made my dick as hard as eating it made yours."

"The cock wants what the cock wants," said Rich idly. "And what my cock has evidently been yearning for is a hearty home-cooked meal."

"Perv," said Jude, rubbing at his cheek, but he didn't think the blush was showing.

He didn't say anything for a while, until Rich asked, "Can you overknead pasta dough?"

"Well, when dough's overkneaded, it becomes hard to work and stretch out, and you don't want that — that's when gluten's basically built up so much that it's stronger than you are. You want enough for a bounce back, but not so much that you can't fight it — but also, uh, with pasta dough, if you have it out for too long, it goes dry."

"What were all the different shapes called?"

"Oh, fuck, okay, so there's the bowties, farfalle, the conchiglie, that's the shells—"

Rich was smiling as he kept going. Jude tried not to think too much about it.

* * *

He spent a lot of Saturday in bed, watching videos about making pasta — people made it in different colours by adding beets or green vegetables, even layered dough made black with squid ink with normal stuff so that the dough you actually ended up with was pinstriped, and there were more shapes than he could even imagine.

He watched challenges where people tried to make as many perfect pieces of pasta as they could in a short period; he watched old Italian grannies showing traditional recipes that had been handed down for generations; he watched a few documentaries about the history of pasta back-to-back.

The whole time, he couldn't help but imagine it under his hands, whenever someone was making it on the screen, what the dough would feel like under his fingers, warm from his own hands kneading it, the texture of it, the weight.

Sunday, he made ravioli stuffed with different cheeses, and when he went to the bar and Rich saw him, his eyes lit up, and he put out his hands.

"Who says I have something?" asked Jude. "Who says it's even for you, if I have?"

"I can *smell* it," said Rich dramatically, and Jude tried to stifle the smile on his face as he reached into his satchel and took out the container, handing it over.

"I like the ricotta and spinach best," he said as they ate the different ravioli together, although Jude didn't eat many from the box, and Rich hummed.

"I like this one, with the... is this bacon?"

"It's pancetta and fried tomato with a little lemon."

"A week in and you're a chef already."

"It's too salty," said Jude.

"That's just the sea air," Rich said dismissively, and put the whole thing in his mouth. He ate with gusto — he was neat and fastidious, was almost as fussy about getting crumbs on himself as Jude was, but he was plainly enjoying it. A little tomato glistened on his lower lip until he licked it away, and Jude could see the bob of his throat as he swallowed.

Maybe it was hot.

Maybe this was Jude's kink now, feeding people.

"What are you cooking this week?"

"Chicken."

"Just chicken?"

"Like ten different ways," said Jude. "But we'll cook everything that goes with the different chicken dishes, the vegetables and stuff — roast, pie, tagine..."

Rich chewed on a raviolo, closed his eyes in his bliss, swallowed. "I look forward to it," he said with relish.

Jude swallowed around nothing.

* * *

It was harder to season a chicken breast than he thought, and harder still not to overcook it so that it dried out but enough that it was fully cooked through; it was hard to butterfly one, and harder still to piece apart a whole chicken with a knife, but when it turned out well, there was a satisfaction in it he couldn't get over.

He loved how it looked once they were finished cooking — because they were doing actual *meals* now more than just staples, Vanessa kept talking about how to plate food like they did in a restaurant, how to portion it out like you were looking at a clock face, how to use angles and contrasting colours to show off the dish, how to place your garnishes.

He was initially terrified of the deep fat fryer and the hot oil that came spitting out of it, but the fried chicken that came out of it was some of the best he'd ever tasted even before he started experimenting with seasoning and spicing the flour, and it left Rich moaning as he bit into it.

"Do you want to get married?" he asked, and Jude laughed.

The question made his stomach twist in his gut, made him suddenly aware of all the blood in his veins, the heart in his chest, but he kept on smiling.

"Broken leg won't make me your fucking housewife."

"I can't offer you half of my ungenerous pay packet and shitty apartment?"

Jude grabbed a piece of the chicken, biting into it, tasted the paprika, the nutmeg, what he now knew was mace, the cumin. He'd spent the last few days tasting all the spices he could find — he'd bought a spice rack, because they didn't have one, and it was full now, with a few boxes of fresh herbs underneath.

Maria had seen, and she'd brought over three little plant pots with clippings from her husband's garden — fresh thyme, basil, and mint, and Jude had been so excited he'd thrown his arms around her and then apologised profusely, but she'd laughed.

He'd tried to give her money for the cuttings, but she wouldn't take it — she'd taken the chicken pot pie he'd made for her and her husband and their son, though, and something inside him had felt wonderful and warm and *big* at being able to cook for her, when she always cooked for them, and especially cooked for Jude.

"I'm scared of the deep fat fryer," he admitted. "We used it a little for making fries, but it's fucking hot."

"Cooking oil? Hot? You astonish me."

"Yeah, I *know*," said Jude. "But I don't want to put my hand in it."

"Good, best not," murmured Rich, nodding wisely. "Very grisly meat on the hand. Better your thigh."

"Ugh."

After they'd eaten everything, Rich sighed, leaning back in his chair with his hand over his stomach. Jude saw the way his palm shifted over the fabric of his shirt and wanted to reach out and touch with his own, wondered how warm Rich's skin was, how much it yielded.

"Why haven't you got a boyfriend?" he asked, and Rich huffed out a laugh.

"You sound like my aunt."

"That mean you don't know?"

"I'm difficult to live with," said Rich. "Opinionated. Fussy. And I'm not good at meeting men — I'm a creature of habit, like to go to the same places and do the same things."

"Why, just because you hang out all the time with a hetero dude with a broken leg?"

"If you were eye candy I might use you as a dick magnet, but unfortunately..." He gestured vaguely at Jude.

He knew it was a joke. He still asked, "Am I really not hot?"

Rich blinked at him, arching an eyebrow, and said, "You're handsome enough. Those lips, that jaw, those eyes, not to mention your muscles. Your arse is nice, although I don't know if women look for that. Why, worried about being single?"

"I'm not good at dating," said Jude. "I don't like having to give up all my time to someone to date them, not having any free time left."

"You know, if dating feels like a chore, I expect it's a sign you're dating the wrong person."

"Every girl I've ever dated has been the wrong one, I guess," Jude muttered, then realised how fucking gay that sounded, and said a little more loudly, "but it's not like I want to get married any time soon."

Rich shrugged, changed the subject.

Jude almost wanted him to go back to it, but he didn't say anything about it.

* * *

His dad and his brothers came back that weekend and he cooked for them, made a bacon-wrapped chicken breast stuffed with cream cheese and spinach. The breasts were a little overcooked, but he gave his dad the best one, and luckily the sauce was thick enough that it wasn't that bad.

"What do you think of the food?" he asked.

His father looked at him, confused. "It's fine," he said.

"Why, is there something wrong with yours?" asked James. "We can call her back, Jude—"

"Maria's already at home by now," muttered Jude, wrinkling his nose, "and she didn't cook it, *I* did."

"You cooked this?" Jonah asked, raising his eyebrows. "Where the fuck did you learn to do that?"

"I've been taking classes," said Jude, and all three of them stared at him. "Look, the fuck else am I gonna do? I'm bored of sitting around drinking beers and jacking off."

"Could learn to do something more useful," said his father in a mutter.

The conversation turned to rising seal populations.

Jude waited for a good time to turn the conversation back to the food, but a good moment didn't come up, so he drank his beer, and let it drop.

* * *

Jude had never really liked pork outside of the occasional piece of ham or bacon, had never really liked lamb that much either, and that didn't change when he was cooking either himself, but Rich groaned with satisfaction around everything Jude brought him.

"You really think I'm good?" he asked.

"I think it's criminal that you didn't break your leg earlier," said Rich around a mouthful of herb-encrusted lamb. "I'm ready to make letting you feed me my full-time obsession."

Jude adjusted his jeans.

"I cooked for my dad," said Jude, mostly to kill his inconvenient boner, and Rich looked at him seriously. Jude's erection rallied admirably as he watched Rich suck lamb juices off his fingers.

"How'd that go?"

"My brothers liked it. But they didn't talk much about it. They thought the housekeeper made it until I said it was me."

"And your father?"

"He said it'd be more useful for me to learn to do something else."

"Fuck useful," said Rich.

"It's not like I could do this as a job," said Jude. "Be a chef."

"Why not?"

"I'm thirty-two, Rich," said Jude.

"Well, you're a terrible deckhand. You're better at this."

Jude laughed, kicked Rich with his good foot. "Did you really come sit with me a few weeks because 'cause it was busy?"

"I thought you were lonely," said Rich quietly. "Like me."

"That's gay as shit."

"It's lonely to be gay," said Rich, as if Jude had meant it seriously. "To be an outsider, an outlier."

"I didn't mean it in a shitty way," muttered Jude. "It's fine that you're gay. Never bothered me — it's not a big deal. I don't think."

Rich nodded his head, and went back to eating. "You're making me gain weight, you know," he said. "I normally don't eat much in the evenings."

Jude did know. Had noticed. Rich had gained a little more bulk in his upper arms, and was thicker around his middle — but mostly, he could see the shift in the shape of his ass, because Rich wore chinos or suit pants most days, wore them tightly tailored, and he was filling them out a lot more these days than he used to.

"Want me to stop feeding you?" Jude asked, feeling like he was on the edge of a cliff, and Rich scoffed.

"*Never*," he said emphatically, and the cliffside feeling evaporated. "I just shudder to think what could have been if you'd taken woodcraft. I can't eat a fucking wooden duck."

Jude laughed, and when Rich grinned, Jude savoured the details of his smile.

* * *

Not that it was anybody's business what he thought about when he jacked off, but when he was in the shower, trying to avoid the crinkling of the plastic around his casted leg, Jude thought about Rich.

He thought about Rich well-fed and healthy with his arse fat and his muscles working, Rich sucking juice and sauce off his fingers until they were clean, Rich with his stomach full of what Jude had made for him. The thoughts spiralled from there, thoughts about feeding Rich right off the fork, or even with his hands, Rich sucking *Jude's* fingers clean, Rich demanding dessert and bending him over and—

He came pretty hard, which was great, but immediately following this he slipped, fell, and smashed his head hard enough on the little towel shelf that the corner of it cut his head open, and blood smeared down the white-painted wood.

He felt sick and dizzy, vision going dark for a second, and he clumsily grabbed for his phone to turn off his music and call the only actual friend he had on the island.

* * *

The lights were very bright in the hospital, and Jude sat there squinting in a hospital gown and the boxers Rich had thrown into the back of his car.

Rich stood there beside them as Jude scowled, feeling the distant pinch of his stitches, something he *knew* about more than he really felt.

"Missed the hospital so much you just had to come back?" asked the nurse, and Jude didn't say anything.

Rich said, "He wants to punch his card enough, earn his tenth x-ray free."

The nurse chuckled. "You're the guy that didn't even flinch when we set your leg in place, right?"

Jude, careful not to move his head as she was working, shrugged his shoulders, and kept his jaw set.

"He takes it like a champ, huh?" she asked Rich.

"I'm sure I wouldn't know," Rich said smoothly, winking at him, and Jude's lip twitched, but he didn't quite smile. His head felt hollow, and he didn't think he could manage it if he tried. "Will you need to do anything with his cast?"

"No, you guys did great keeping it dry."

"Is it hurting you?" asked Rich. "Your leg?"

"No."

"Your head?"

"Nah."

"Just your ego that's bruised, hm?"

"Mostly, yeah," said Jude.

The nurse looked awkward. He felt distantly bad, was sure he was meant to be making conversation, small talk, meant to say *something*, but what the fuck was he meant to say?

"Is he the first naked patient you've had this week?" asked Rich.

"Not even the first we've had tonight, I'm afraid," said the nurse, and Rich sighed.

"And after all this pageantry, just for this display of public indecency, Jude, none of them will even remember you."

Jude stared at him, lips still feeling a little dead, but he said — his voice was slightly hoarse, and he wondered if they could tell — "They'll remember. This ass is a work of art."

The nurse laughed, and Rich smiled at him, gave a nod of his head.

It was easier to let Rich do the talking, and Rich did from then on, making smooth and easy conversation with her without prompting Jude to join in. He knew her name, Jude realised, and he knew the name of the doctor he saw too. He asked questions about how his pain meds would interact with his topical anaesthetic, what antibiotics he'd need to take if there were signs of infection, when the stitches would dissolve.

"You know all about how to look after a concussion, Mr Chastain," said the nurse. "Can you look after him?"

"Of course," said Rich, not even hesitating, not even looking at Jude to *ask*, and something about it made Jude feel happy and empty all at once.

"Thanks," he said in Rich's car, with a blanket in his lap from one of the pockets on the back of the seat. He wanted to say more, he knew he should, but he didn't. Couldn't.

"It's nothing," Rich said mildly. "I hope you don't mind if I stay with you for a few hours."

"It's fine," said Jude.

"You can cook for me," said Rich.

Jude felt himself smile, and then forced it down. "Sure," he said.

Once they were inside and he was working pasta dough under his fingers, he asked, "Were you working?"

Rich was sitting back at the kitchen chair, sipping at a glass of red wine Jude had picked out of the rack at random.

"No, it's my day off," said Rich. "I was painting."

"You paint?"

"Not art," said Rich. "I paint those little figurines, you know, the ones they use for model trains, tabletop games. My cousin runs a game shop, and he buys them unpainted second-hand, for cheap, then paints them. I do some of them too — they sell for a decent amount, I'm told, but I just find it calming."

"You like that nerd shit?" asked Jude, and Rich shrugged his shoulders.

"Not particularly. I did one or two models when I was a teenager, of ships, that sort of thing, but I'm not that into displaying them, and I'm not really into the games or anything. I mostly paint soldiers and normal people — he does elves and dragons and orcs and such, but I can't make head nor tail of all that. I just like painting them: it's relaxing."

"Are you good at it?"

"Oh, yes. I have a very steady hand, and I'm good at uniform details on all the little coloniser uniforms — you know, the Brits, the French, the Dutch, the Belgians. All those gold buttons and epaulettes. I don't tend to do things I'm not good at, Jude. I'm too much of an egotist."

Jude had never talked to anybody before who talked about themselves like Rich did, who seemed to know themselves the way Rich did. It made him feel raw just to witness it, like an exposed nerve.

"What pasta are you making?" Rich asked.

"Tortellini," said Jude. "I made a stock from leftover chicken, I'm not sure how good it is. I've never made stock before, so you have to tell me if the broth is shit."

"I doubt I'll need to."

"I like pasta," mumbled Jude, shifting his weight slightly — he was a little hazy from his meds, disconnected enough from his body he didn't feel his leg or the new stitches in his head, and he wanted to make sure he didn't put too much weight on the cast.

"Good," said Rich. "It's good to have things we like."

"Can I tell you something?"

"No. I'm going to put my fingers in my years and sing *La Bamba* as loud as I can so that I can't hear you."

"Dick."

"I prefer Rich."

"I've watched like two hundred pasta videos the past few weeks. More, maybe. It's like... my new obsession."

"That," said Rich, swilling his wine in his glass, "is adorable. Possibly the most adorable thing I've ever heard."

"Would you shut the fuck up?"

"A man can't voice his opinion?"

"I've just never felt this way about something before, that's all. It makes me feel good just to think about making pasta. Makes me smile. Makes me feel calm. Is that weird?"

"You didn't like food before?" Rich asked, and Jude considered the question as he passed his dough through the machine, the first thing he'd bought after coming out of class.

"I did," Jude said, and it was true. He liked nice restaurants, liked to try new things, especially if it was a group dinner and he knew he wouldn't be talking much, but that everyone else would be too busy talking to each other to bother him or ask him questions.

He vaguely remembered having a toy kitchen when he was a kid, remembered having wooden utensils and a chef's hat and an apron. He also distantly recalled having it taken off him, remembered being shouted at on one occasion for playing with his stupid girls' toys instead of…

He didn't even remember.

It hadn't even been about that, really, had just been because his mom had bought it for him, and his dad hadn't liked it. He remembered playing with his brothers instead, or doing sports. He'd never wanted to row at school or play sports either, but his dad had insisted on it.

He didn't think anyone made a big deal of taking home ec classes, but he remembered joking with his brothers. He never even considered signing up for it, knew it'd be like putting a big sign on his back that said "homo".

"When'd you know you were gay?" asked Jude.

"Always," said Rich. "Since I was a child I knew something. That I was different. I understood how later on — that I liked boys the way other boys liked girls, that I had a natural flair for fashion, a sort of charm and internal beauty most other men couldn't compare to."

Jude started laughing, giving Rich a look halfway between admiring and disgusted. "Do you *hear* yourself?"

"I do, I do," said Rich. "I like to listen to myself talk, and admire myself in mirrors, too."

"Fucking cockatoo."

"A homophobic slur that ought be brought into the limelight."

"Cockatoo is *not* a slur."

"It should be. It has the word *cock* and everything."

Jude's face felt warm and relaxed from smiling, like freshly worked dough. "You knew you were gay when you started puberty?"

"Mmm, before. By the time I was eight, nine. That was when I started noticing other boys, but I didn't have my first kiss until I was sixteen. I always knew I wasn't attracted to women, and my parents both suspected from when I was very young and made sure I saw examples, so there was no real crisis for me. My father's really quite a..."

"He's not quiet, you know, he's very communicative, but he's not incredibly comfortable talking about prejudice, about bigotry, about identity from a vulnerable position. He takes a defensive position, you know, expects a fight — for him, pride comes from a place of viciously defending what is under attack. He's not wrong to feel that way, but he thinks the loving part can go unsaid and still be as strong. He and my mother were at odds on that — as are he and I."

"That's about... about race, though, right? Not... not being gay?"

"My father isn't gay, no."

"Well, *no*, obviously. But he's..." Jude didn't know what the right words were. "Like you."

"Like me," echoed Rich, seeming amused.

"Mestizo?"

Rich coughed around his drink, laughing, and he shook his head, swilling what was in his mouth and swallowing. "Who taught you that? You didn't learn that word in New York."

"I've lived here as much all my life as I have in New York," muttered Jude, looking down at his pasta. "Maria uses it, anyway."

"Maria?"

"She cleans here a few times a week, and cooks for us sometimes. She's Mexican, and her husband's from El Salvador. It's a bad word?"

"No, not in this context," said Rich. "It just took me by surprise, that's all. It's probably accurate to apply it to me, and my family. My mother was from Caracas, and my father was born and raised on Martinique. Half of everyone born in these islands, around these seas, has some native blood in them, one way or another."

"But your dad is Black," said Jude. "You have those eyes from your mother's side." Rich laughed, but he didn't look that happy, and Jude said, "Sorry. I didn't mean— Sorry. That's rude."

"Yes," Rich agreed.

"Sorry."

"You're all white Irish New Yorkers since your ancestors emigrated from the Emerald Isle, I suppose?"

"My mom's mom is Scottish," said Jude, with a small, uncertain smile, and he was relieved when Rich's next laugh was more relaxed.

"Forgive me for assuming," said Rich. "I should have guessed at such familial diversity just to look at you."

Jude smiled slightly.

"I first kissed a boy when I was sixteen, I told you," said Rich. "You're avoiding the question."

"I'm not gay," said Jude. "I don't kiss men."

"Okay," said Rich. "Presumably you've kissed women, though."

"Oh," said Jude. He tried to concentrate on the pasta. "I first kissed a girl when I was like fourteen," he said once he started folding the tortellini, neatly stuffing each pouch of pasta and making it wasn't too full, wasn't stuffed too tightly. He liked how it felt, liked how he had to be delicate but firm with each one, moulding them with his fingers.

"Was it good?" asked Rich. "Mine wasn't. He cut my lip open with his braces, and our glasses kept clicking together."

Jude laughed, trying to imagine it — he remembered the glasses Rich had worn at school now that Rich said it, and they weren't that big, but he guessed even small glasses were hard if you were both wearing them.

"It was fine. It was... wet." Sloppy. And she'd cried, after — he'd said the wrong thing. Upset her. "You fuck a lot?"

"I have a premium Grindr account, so I suppose you could call me something of a whore. I put in good hours — I rather deserve a spot on the list of five-star tourist attractions, I think."

"I don't know what the fuck that means."

"Well, I suck a lot of—"

"The account thing."

"Grindr? It's a hook-up app for men."

"Oh," said Jude. "Right."

It wasn't the answer he expected, the answer he wanted. He couldn't have imagined that answer. He thought about rich fucking dudes, random tourists, Rich naked, Rich sucking dick and smearing come on his lips, Rich kissing.

Rich eating pasta and sitting on Jude's—

"What, you only make love?" asked Rich amusedly. "No casual fucks for Saint Jude?"

"I fuck," muttered Jude. "At parties and shit, not on apps. I just get hammered and have a good time."

"You never have sex sober?" asked Rich.

Jude realised with a distant lurch that he hadn't.

"Nothing wrong if you don't like sex," said Rich evenly, with a gentleness to his tone that Jude didn't know what to do with. "Not everyone even enjoys it, you know — not everyone considers it worth the effort. For some people, sex is only a chore, or even just something mildly pleasant but not worth working for, something they engage in mostly for the benefit of others."

"I'm not a fucking eunuch, Rich."

"I'm not saying you are! Just that some people feel they absolutely must have sex, that they're not masculine without it, or that they're somehow inhuman if they don't care for it. You don't have to fuck anyone just to match up to some sort of outside expectation."

"You psychoanalysing me just to say I only fuck girls at parties to impress my dad?"

Rich kept looking at him, unflinching. "Do you?"

"Ugh."

Jude cooked his pasta.

The broth tasted good when he made it, salty but in a way that made it feel more satisfying, and the tortellini, packed with a pork mince fried with tomato and some garlic cloves and stuff, is good. He thought maybe he overcooked the filling, because it felt slightly dry on his tongue even with the broth, but Rich still ate blissfully.

"You like food too much," said Jude.

"I don't give a fuck," said Rich, chewing around one of the pasta parcels and then groaning quietly. "I could eat your cooking 'til I fucking ripped at the seams."

Jude swallowed, and sipped his drink.

"Some people don't like sex, but like things like that," said Rich. "Bondage, roleplay, dress-up, whatever — or feeding their partner."

"You fucking saying I get off on this?" Jude demanded, voice so loud it rattled in the room — as per usual, Rich didn't even blink.

"I'm more just making conversation," said Rich. "I don't know much about it, but I don't know that people always *get off* on it, so to speak. For some of them it's a mental stimulation, not an orgasm. Some people have a fetish for balloons."

This was such a nonsequitur that Jude didn't know how to be indignant about it. "Balloons? Like... like balloons, balloons? Fucking a balloon?"

"It depends on the person, I think. Enjoying the balloon, its texture, the sound, the pop — or imagining inflatable people. Toys."

"Is this what you fucking think about all day when you're meant to be deciding what boat docks where?" asked Jude, and Rich laughed around another mouthful of pasta.

"It crosses my mind from time to time," he admitted. "You can't understand other people if you can't understand yourself — and ditto vice versa. I like to try to understand what makes people tick."

"I don't understand anybody," said Jude. "Seems to me like everyone looks like they're one thing and actually they're something else. And there's rules, but only some people get punished for not following them."

"What rules?"

"Like you don't know."

Rich shrugged. "Maybe I don't."

"Sometimes I feel like all of this time you spend with me is some elaborate set-up to trick me into fucking you," said Jude. "And everyone sees it except me, because I'm just... stupid, and you know I'm stupid, especially compared to you."

He wanted Rich to get angry at him, wanted him to yell, to punch him, maybe.

Instead, Rich looked at him interestedly, like he'd posed some kind of prompt for a debate, and asked, "Do you always think of gay men as inherently predatory?"

Jude stared at him. "What? No," he said hurriedly.

"It's something about me, then?"

"No, shit, no."

Rich said, after a few moments of quiet between them, said, "I don't want to trick you into anything, or want you to do anything you don't want. We're friends — I thought so, anyway. I'd like to think the both of us want to see the other man happy, no matter what that entails."

"Do you think I'm gay?" asked Jude.

"You keep telling me you're not."

"What, you think I'm in denial?"

"That's not my call to make."

"You want me to suck your dick though?" Jude demanded. He felt angry and naked, backed into a corner and vulnerable and pressed up on, and that Rich was so calm made it worse.

"I'm not the sort of man to turn down a free blowjob," said Rich cleanly, "but the amount of anger coming off you isn't the sort of thing that encourages a man to put any of his intimate parts near your mouth. Why do you bring it up, do you want to suck my cock?"

"No!"

"Is this some sort of reverse psychological method of getting me to suck yours?"

Jude felt himself burn with guilt, shame. "Fucking, no, I'm not... I wouldn't expect you to do, to do that. Wouldn't ask."

Rich laughed, a quiet chuckle. "I'm not saying I wouldn't enjoy it, if you did."

Jude stared down at his empty bowl, hard as fuck and trying desperately not to freak out entirely.

"We're adults, Jude," said Rich. "As far as I see it, sex is just sex. It doesn't have to mean the world — and having sex with a man or a woman isn't what makes you gay or straight or in-between or something else. That's what you *are*, how you feel about men and women, your emotion, your attraction, your sexuality. Sex itself doesn't determine your identity any more than masturbation does." He inhaled, and then said, a little more gently, "Would you like me to?"

Jude swallowed. Couldn't think, couldn't talk.

Rich stood, leaned over the table, and gave Jude all the forewarning in the world: he cupped Jude's jaw very carefully, tilted his head up, met his gaze before their lips touched. His lips were firm, warm, slightly slick with chapstick, and when his tongue slid against Jude's...

The sound that came out of Jude's mouth was indescribable, a harsh, desperate whine he'd never made any other time, and he put his hands on Rich's body like he was drowning and Rich was a life raft, pulling him closer, kissing him hard. He slid his hands under his shirt and touched his belly, his sides, feeling where he was muscular and where he was solid and where he was soft, his head spinning with the knowledge that at least some of this belly, some of these hips, *he'd* made.

It was because of the meds, he thought, that it was so overwhelming, his skin on fire, the whole of him sensitive and wanting and *fuck*, it was nothing like being drunk, nothing like any hurried thing he'd ever done with a girl. He didn't mean to close his eyes but they were closed, his nostrils full of the scent of Rich's expensive shampoo, and it was everything, *everything*—

The noise he made next was like a fucking squeak, the kind of noise a fucking teenager would make, and maybe that was fitting, because.

Because.

It felt good, of course it felt good, but he was so embarrassed he could fucking die. Rich pulled away from his lips, mouthing over his jaw in a way that made Jude's eyes roll up in his head. His tone was painfully smug as he asked, "Did you just...?"

"Shut up."

"No blowjobs on the table today, then."

"More," Jude begged, and Rich kept kissing him.

"You need another shower," he said when they finally stopped kissing. Jude was drenched in sweat, his shirt sticking to his chest, his boxers wet and uncomfortable as fuck in his shirts.

"I can't believe I did that," he moaned.

"If it helps," said Rich, "the fact that with kisses alone I made a man my age cream himself is an inordinate compliment, and quite the boost to my ego."

"You don't need compliments or boosts to your ego," said Jude. "And please never call it that again."

"Inordinate praise?" Rich suggested, and Jude shoved him in the side. "You want me to go?"

"You want to go?"

"No. I'd like to stay, watch a movie. Unless you want me to leave so you can panic in private."

"I'm not panicking," said Jude. He felt like he might, later.

"Good," Rich murmured.

Lying on the couch an hour later, Jude kept a gap between him and Rich, didn't touch him, until Rich asked, "Do you mind if I touch you?"

Jude's tongue wouldn't work, so he shrugged his shoulders. Rich reached out and started stroking his hair, the back of his neck. His fingertips played hard enough that it didn't tickle, and just felt nice, really nice.

It was good in a way that made Jude want to crawl under a rock, tear his skin off, scream at the sky — it was good in a way that was mild and far too much at once, and he sat there, hunkered down, stiff as a board.

"Want me to stop?" Rich asked quietly. He was leaning forward, his pale eyes moving back and forth as he studied Jude's face.

Jude couldn't make his mouth move. He shrugged.

Rich gave a very small nod, kept stroking up and down his neck, his fingers moving through the back of Jude's short-cropped hair and then back down between his shoulder blades. He quietly sighed at the pressure on the muscle.

"Thanks," he whispered.

"We never have to do anything you don't want to," said Rich. "We can have sex, or not. Kiss, or not. Whatever you want, which includes nothing."

"I don't know how to be gay," said Jude.

"Well, you didn't know how to cook a month ago," Rich pointed out, and Jude laughed.

"Know any classes I can take?"

"Mmm," Rich murmured, leaning closer, "I can recommend a private tutor."

Jude closed the gap between them, kissed Rich, and when Rich sighed in pleasure into his mouth it was incredible. *He'd* made Rich make that sound, *he* did that – and now, he swallowed it.

* * *

They were lying in bed, Jude on his back, absently stroking his fingers over the top of his cast, and Rich was lying on his side beside him. They'd been talking about Rich's work for a while, the various crises of the day.

"Can I touch you?" Rich asked, and Jude nodded almost before he'd finished asking the question, one small, tight movement.

Rich shifted closer on the bed, curling himself against Jude's side.

"I worry I'm overwhelming you," said Rich quietly. "Am I?"

"Yeah," said Jude. "Like... like a hot bath. It's a lot, but I just, I want, I need..." He couldn't say it, couldn't say anything, but when Rich curled an arm around his belly, Jude grasped at it tightly, pressed his fingertips into the meat of Rich's arm.

"Sleep?" he asked.

Jude kissed him, and there was something searing about the way Rich kissed him back, something so hot about it that it felt scalding, sanctifying.

Too much.

He slept deeper in bed with Rich beside him than he ever had in all his life.

They showered together in the morning, and it was simultaneously the most incredibly erotic experience of his life while not actually being that sexual at all — Rich washed his hair and scrubbed his back, kept kissing him under the spray of the shower, and it felt wonderful and luxurious and *hot...*

But touching Rich back felt almost religious. Being able to run his fingers over Rich's skin, over his chest, his belly, being able to pull a washcloth over the backs of his heavy shoulders and see the way the white suds of soap built up and were then washed away, down his back.

"No tattoos," said Jude. "No scars."

"I'm the picture of perfection," said Rich, but then he leaned down and pressed a kiss to the sun tattooed over Jude's heart, slid his palm around the mermaid on his side, turned Jude to the side so he could kiss the face of the Virgin Mary on his upper arm. "But this is pretty perfect, too."

"We can't both be perfect," said Jude.

"Of course we can," purred Rich, and when his hands slotted into place on each of Jude's hips, resting against his waist like they belonged there, Jude's head spun. "Relax, I'll show you how."

He swallowed, and Rich kissed his Adam's apple, making it bob again.

* * *

"You *are* gaining weight," said Jude a week and a half later.

He was staring at Rich, which was what he mostly had been doing, these past weeks — he didn't feel like he could reach out and touch him the way that Rich touched him, even though Rich always asked first. He'd learned to make excuses to stand closer, to sit closer, to just sort of be there *next* to him, and after a little while Rich would close the gap and touch him, put their shoulders together, or touch their feet together, or hold his hand, or touch his hair.

It was hard.

He couldn't steel himself to touch Rich unless Rich touched him first, but the idea of saying it out loud, trying to wrap his mouth around words that said, "I'm a fucking baby, please touch me, please pay attention to me" made his skin crawl.

It wasn't like dating a girl, he didn't think, but he'd never really dated much — his brothers had dated different girls here and there, and James had been engaged twice to the same girl, breaking up with her again each time. Jude never had, really. He'd meet girls, talk to them, go on group dates, but that was... it.

They did the same things you were meant to on dates.

Drank.

Jude fed Rich.

Rich gave Jude rides.

They talked about Jude's classes, and Rich's work, and about sailing, diving, swimming.

A few nights Rich stayed over after work, and they kissed, but not anything else. Jude wasn't sure if he should feel guilty about the fact that they'd just kiss for hours like teenagers, wondered if Rich would get annoyed, impatient, but he never seemed to.

Rich asked him before he kissed him, touched him, played with his hair, his shoulders, but he didn't ask if he could touch Jude's dick or his ass.

"Do you think my dick is small?" asked Jude.

"It's a little above average for this area," said Rich.

"What, so that makes yours huge?"

Rich laughed. "Mine's not that much bigger than yours. It's about the same girth, anyway, and mine's not more than an inch longer."

"That makes you top though," said Jude uncertainly, glancing back at him, and Rich met his gaze.

"I'm vers, actually."

"Vers?"

"I like to top, I like to bottom," said Rich. "I like to suck and be sucked... I like other things. Mutual masturbation — I like frottage, you know what that is? Both of us grinding our cocks against one another?"

Jude shook the frying pan, trying to make sure nothing stuck as it fried, and Rich watched him with interest. Jude could always feel when Rich was watching him, even though he couldn't always handle making eye contact.

He remembered kids would bully Rich sometimes at school, making fun of how light his eyes were, how spooky it made him look, but it wasn't that — Jude liked Rich's eyes, and they were as beautiful as the rest of him, it was just that they were attached to Rich, and Rich was smart, and Jude wasn't. Rich knew everything, and Jude knew basically nothing.

He didn't feel *scared* of Rich, nothing as stupid as that — he trusted him.

It just seemed shitty that Rich kept having to deal with him.

"I don't actually especially like anal," said Rich. "A lot of men prefer to have it, so I've had a good amount of it, but it's by no means my favourite activity. I wouldn't miss it, is what I'm saying, if you'd rather not try it."

"What, and just not have real sex?" asked Jude, his voice breaking a little on the last word.

"My mouth feels fairly real, I think. Ditto my hands. There's frottage, as I said — intercrural, intergluteal - hotdogging. Toys."

"I know what like half of that is," said Jude.

"Cock against cock. Fucking between the thighs, fucking between the buttocks."

"Sounds messy."

"Everything fun always is."

Jude stared down at the pop and sizzle of the sesame oil in the pan. "Do you think I'm a pussy?"

"I've never seen one face to face," Rich admitted. "I wouldn't know, I've no basis of comparison."

Jude gave him a very sour look. "You really think you're funny, don't you?"

"From time to time, I certainly do. Keep it close to your chest, though. My comedy stylings are a well-kept secret." When Jude didn't say anything, staring down at the frying pan, Rich said, "I don't think you're a coward. I think you're repressed and inexperienced — I think you have difficulties expressing yourself, and I'm not about to speculate as to why or what the causes of that are, but I think that your issues with it are quite extreme. The difference between the man I met in the pub, the man on his guard with a stranger, and the man in front of me now, the man that you are in private, is... not what I would have expected."

"You think I'm crazy?"

"Did I say that?" Rich asked. "I don't think you're crazy. I think you're... shy. Anxious. I find it hard to tell what you're thinking, what you're feeling, at times — but I get the impression, and correct me if I'm wrong, that you find it hard to tell the same in everyone else."

Jude didn't say anything. He felt like he could hear wind rushing in his ears.

"I think you're even more nervous about your inexperience with me, with men, than you otherwise would be, because of your age. It's all compounded by that sense that your life's about to be over, but Jude, you're the same age I am — neither of us is on the verge of death because we're past thirty. We've probably both got two thirds of our lives yet to come."

"My dad was a captain by the time he was my age," said Jude.

"There's something to be said for nepotism, I suppose," said Rich.

Jude grabbed the tongs to put the stirfry into two bowls — the noodles were fresh, and they tasted good, but it was hard to get the textures right on different vegetables. The more he practised, the more he'd be able to get the timing right, he thought.

"Our manifest says your father is back in port tomorrow," said Rich.

"Yeah."

"I haven't told anyone in town about us, you know. Gossip shouldn't reach them — for all they might know, there's been no escalation in our relationship."

Jude was quiet. Rich ate with his customary enthusiasm, and it gave him time to think, to mull over exactly what he wanted to say.

"Do you think I want to keep it secret?" asked Jude, so quietly he almost couldn't hear it himself. "You think I'm... ashamed of you?"

"I think," said Rich in a slow, considered way, "that I don't have much to lose. My family knows about me, and I'm a renowned faggot, have been since I was a teenager."

Jude flinched when he said the word, didn't know why he did when he'd said it himself often enough, and there was a slightly pained expression in Rich's face when he saw his reaction.

"My orientation is established, is what I'm trying to say," said Rich. "But this is *your* life, Jude. I'm not going to force you to out yourself to your family, especially if you're not even sure that this is right for you."

"You're right for me."

Rich hesitated, his hand hovering over the table, but then it slowly enclosed Jude's, and Jude felt himself relax.

"Isn't it shitty of me?" asked Jude. "Didn't you come out because you didn't want to be someone's dirty secret?"

"I don't think I ever formally came out," said Rich. "I just sucked cock prodigiously and people came to their own conclusions. Would you like to try that?"

Jude started laughing, harder than he meant to, and he coughed into his arm to keep from spitting shredded carrot everywhere. "Yeah," he mumbled, clearing his throat. "I'll consider it."

"But in a really manly way," Rich assured him. "You'll be very masc about the fellatio."

"Right," said Jude, smiling. "Masc."

* * *

"You cook this?" his father asked over the table.

Jude smiled as he looked up, but then he saw his dad's serious expression, and the smile evened out into nothing. "Yep," he said, meeting the old man's stare and steeling himself to keep from flinching.

"It's fucking *great*," said James, and Jonah tapped his agreement against the table, because his mouth was full of lamb chop.

"What are we paying Maria extra for if you're cooking everything?"

Her son's going to a new school, and the extra money helps, Jude didn't say.

"That mean you don't like it?" he asked.

His dad sighed, pinching the bridge of his nose. "Is this going to be a new thing with you?" he demanded. "Fucking around cooking all the time? Haven't you got enough distractions to contend with?"

"Like what?" asked Jude.

His dad went very cool, leaning back in his seat, and Jude kept staring at him even though he felt like throwing up. "You think you can talk back to me because you can't sail?" he asked: his voice was a low, gruff rumble, and it made Jude's stomach give an anxious flip, but he knew better than to look away. Looking away, flinching, that always got you something much worse.

"I'm not talking back," he said thinly. "I'm just asking what else you want me to do."

"This cooking thing is a waste of time," he said. "How will you use this when you're back on deck? Where's the transferable skill? What, when you finally stop fucking around and get married, are you gonna be Mr Mom, do all the cooking and cleaning while she works? That your new career plan?"

Jude thought about that for a second, imagined sitting at home, looking after a kid, waiting for Rich to finish at work. He thought about teaching a kid how to tie knots, how to bake and cook — thought about having dinner waiting on the table when Rich came in the door.

It was a more appealing thought than being married to a woman ever had been, for no reason he currently wanted to consider in detail.

"You talk back," his dad said sharply, "and now you ignore me."

"Maybe I'm not good at sailing," said Jude. "Maybe I'd be better at something else — like this."

"Maybe if you put your head down instead of fucking around pretending to be a housewife, you'd be a better deckhand."

Jude didn't say anything.

He knew Rich would. Rich would rip his father a new asshole without even hesitating — what would Rich say? Ask if he hates women? Ask what he has against housewives if he's so desperate for his sons to have them, if he's scared of not controlling his son? If all this anxiety is because *his* ex-housewife is a career woman that's more successful than he ever was now?

James and Jonah started the conversation back up, and Jude stayed quiet — it was always easier to let them pick up the slack, let them take up the attention, fade into the background.

Everyone cleared their plate but him.

"Can I stay at yours?" he asked on the phone as Jonah loaded the dishwater.

"Of course, always," said Rich. "You want me to pick you up or send a taxi over?"

"I can drive you, bro," said James behind him.

Jude looked at him, and James gave him a smile, an encouraging nod. "You hear that?" asked Jude.

"Sure. See you in twenty."

As Jude picked up his satchel, which had his meds and a change of clothes in it, his father asked, "You going out?"

"Sleepover," said Jude.

"Who is she?" asked his father immediately. "Do we know her?"

"I don't know," said Jude, and kept going on his crutches down the stairs.

"You're gonna get your ass beat, talking back to the old man like that," said James, and Jude shrugged, pulling the passenger door of his brother's car open and dropping inside.

"I don't give a shit," said Jude. "Old man wants to beat me, he can try. Thanks for the ride."

"I want to get a look at this girl. She in your cooking class?"

Jude shook his head, and he gave directions as James frowned, guessed different women it could be. When they pulled up outside the house split into two flats, Rich's little smart car outside, James frowned.

"She a yachtie?"

"Nah."

"She's not rich."

"No."

Rich came out onto the balcony, wine glass in hand, waved, and turned to go back inside to head downstairs and come out via the front door.

"Was that... Is that Richard Chastain?"

"Yeah."

"The gay kid from St Nick's? The one that got expelled after he broke into their principal's office and took all his furniture apart?"

Jude started laughing. "Was that him?"

James was staring at him.

"I didn't know that was him," said Jude, and opened the door.

"What, you're fucking gay now?" asked James, leaning over the gearstick to stare at him. Jude didn't know what to make of his expression. "That why you picked up this cooking thing? Because you're dating him?"

"I don't know," said Jude, and then said again, "Thanks for the ride."

"Hi, James," said Rich when James rolled the window down.

"Richard."

"Enjoy dinner?"

"Yeah, he's pretty good," said James. "You turning my brother into a galley chef?"

Rich shrugged easily, smoothly. "I just give him a ride from classes sometimes," he said.

"And eats the result," added Jude, limping up the path.

"G'night, James," said Rich when Jude didn't. "Thanks for driving him over."

"It's no big deal," said James. "Look after him for us, will you?"

"Always," said Rich.

Jude wondered what James would say to Jonah, what he'd say to Dad, if he'd say anything at all.

Rich put his hand on Jude's lower back as he reached past him to push the door open, and Jude smiled, leaned back into his arm. Rich's lips brushed his shoulder before he ushered him inside.

"It went badly?" he asked.

"Were you the guy that broke into the St Nick's head's office and broke all his furniture?"

Rich blinked, and then laughed. "Yeah," he said. "Two guys on the rowing team were fucking with me, and I got into it with them, but he only punished me. Said I earned it, acting like a fruit — prick was a racist, too."

"You got expelled for that."

"I never meant to get caught."

Jude dropped back onto Rich's bed, and Rich undid his boot for him and put it aside as Jude unbuttoned his shirt.

"How old were you?"

"Sixteen. My father was pretty far out, couldn't reach him on sat phone. He was furious when he got back."

"'Cause you'd been expelled?"

"'Cause they'd had the gall to expel me. He doesn't live here anymore, Ralph Keane, the old principal. There's barely a boat around that'll give him passage because my dad went around telling everyone not to, not just on this island, but loads of the others — he couldn't get his car fixed, couldn't hire a cleaner or a cook, couldn't rent a boat, couldn't even get served in half the bars and restaurants around. He ended up going back to Amsterdam."

Jude was quiet as he slid off his shirt and raised his hips so that Rich could pull his shorts down.

"I don't know if James will tell him," said Jude. "My dad. We don't talk about stuff like that. I don't. Can't. It's... hard. To talk about some stuff. To, to talk about... You know. You know I can't talk much."

Rich kissed his good knee. Jude stared down at him, down on his knees, touching the waistband of Jude's boxers. He couldn't breathe, staring down at him, felt like they were the only two people in all the world.

"You want me to ask you?" Rich asked, finger sliding over the band of his boxers. "I don't want to touch you without making sure you're comfortable, that you're alright with what I'm doing. Is it okay if I ask?"

"Yeah."

"May I suck your cock?"

Jude opened his mouth but no sound came out: he clenched his hands in the sheets either side of him, set his jaw. He couldn't even try to make fun of Rich for the way he'd said it, felt so tense he almost couldn't move at all. He gave the tiniest nod, the only nod he could manage.

Rich's smile was warm and encouraging, and Jude didn't feel like he could possibly deserve it.

Later, Jude laid on his side behind Rich, stroking his back, massaging his shoulders. He wasn't as good at it as Rich was, didn't have the same strength in his hands or the same level of practice, but Rich still moaned when Jude pressed on the knots of muscle he found there.

"He said I'm wasting my time," said Jude. "That I should be studying something more educational — more transferrable skills."

"Did you mention your recent foray into homosexuality?"

"No."

"I'm educational and transferrable."

"He said all I was doing was preparing to be a fucking housewife," said Jude. "That I'd end up playing Mr Mom."

"Strong talk, coming from a man who could be the last father on earth and still not win father of the year."

Jude smiled. "I knew you'd have said something," he said lowly. "I didn't say anything. I just... took it." He hesitated, and then he shifted forward, pressed his face to the back of Rich's neck, put his nose in Rich's hair, curled against his back. "Don't you feel like I'm not worth it?" he asked quietly. "Isn't it too much work? Because I'm... fucked up, and weird, and repressed, and I don't know anything. Not even that I'm not woke like you are, and say shitty stuff, but just that I don't know... *anything.*"

"Jude," Rich murmured.

"I'm not good at wanting you the way you want me," he said. "Not good at making you feel... wanted. It's not fair."

"I'm not grading your performance, Jude. You're here: that's enough."

Jude slept like that, laid on Rich's back, and when he woke up, he was holding him more solidly, his arms curled around him, holding Rich to his chest.

"Desserts this week," said Rich blissfully as the sun rose and shone in through the gaps in his blinds.

Jude laughed, and squeezed him.

* * *

"Oh my fucking *God*," Rich moaned around a forkful of chocolate soufflé, which had risen but then collapsed — they were Jude's nemesis, and while he didn't think the soufflé was going to overtake pasta in his affections, he absolutely wanted to keep practising making them until they turned out well.

"It's good," said Jude. "That you..." He cleared his throat. "Enjoy things."

"You like that I enjoy things?"

"Mm."

"Enjoy food, enjoy cock?" Rich's eyes were shining, his mouth twisted in a grin.

Jude's cheeks were blisteringly hot, and his gut flipped. He couldn't manage words, and grunted out another, "Mm."

"Want to feed me and fuck me all at once? Fill me up to the brim?" Rich's expression was playful, lips curled into a small smile, eyebrows raised, and it made Jude fidget in his seat. "What about it?" he asked, sliding a fork through the soufflé and bringing it up to his mouth, humming as his lips closed around the fork's tines. "Want to fatten me up? See me all a mess?"

"You don't get messy," said Jude.

"No," Rich agreed. "But you like to feed me. Like to please me, like to bring me gifts, make me happy with something you've eaten. To nurture me, care for me. See how happy it makes me that you care."

Jude swallowed hard. He couldn't nod to that, but he evidently didn't need to, because Rich laughed, and his foot touched against Jude's under the table, sliding against his ankle.

"Bet you'd like for me to take a few days off and just lie back for you to wait on me," Rich said experimentally, his eyes narrowing slightly. "Lie in bed, let you feed me everything you feel like cooking, so much so that I can barely eat another bite, can't even button my trousers closed."

Jude stared at him, and Rich went on, "And you'd come rub my stomach for me, wouldn't you? Say sorry that it hurts, but you just want to make me happy? Suck my cock while I'm powerless beneath you, all full up with you and only you, so happy I could burst?"

Jude pushed the heel of his hand down against his half-hard cock, insanely glad that they were at home right now instead of out in the bar, and Rich grinned at him, sliding his foot further up his ankle.

"Yeah," he managed to say, breathlessly, the word barely audible.

"You mind if I ride your cock tonight?" asked Rich, so casually, so easily. "If you're up to giving anal a try."

Jude blinked a few times, rubbing at his cheeks. He thought he managed to nod, but later, he couldn't remember.

Jude slept very, very well that night.

* * *

"You know," said Vanessa on Thursday, watching Jude try his best to drizzle chocolate over the little globes he'd made — pastry was fucking hard, and some of them had come apart while he was picking them out of the mould, and tempering chocolate was... also hard.

He liked that it had such clear, defined boundaries, that it was about specific temperatures, but you still had to stir it right, make sure you didn't fuck it up.

"I know?" repeated Jude.

"You're good at this."

"Thanks."

"What made you take classes? You want official certification for your CV?"

Jude was quiet for a second, frowning as he glanced at her. "I dunno," he said. "Don't have much of a resumé, I guess."

"How much experience do you have cooking? Before this?"

"I don't."

He felt uncomfortable with the look on Vanessa's face, her wide eyes.

"You serious?" she asked.

He nodded.

"Okay, then you're *really* good," she said. "Your basic skills need work — your knife skills, and you're slow to plate, slow to do most stuff, but getting faster is just about practice. What made you take this class?"

"Wanted something to do."

"You this good at everything you do?"

"Ha," said Jude. "Lady, I'm not good at anything."

Vanessa laughed, and said, "Well, you're good at this."

He didn't say anything else, hoping she'd go away, but she didn't, just stuck around and watched him work, watched him burn with embarrassment, feeling like her words were sticking to his back.

"You practice at the weekend?" she asked.

"Yeah."

"You enjoy it? Cooking?"

"Yeah."

"What's your favourite part?"

His jaw hurt from clenching it so hard. "Pasta."

"Pasta?" she repeated, sounding excited, like she had an in, and he swallowed as he kept trying to drizzle the chocolate, trying to get the movement of his wrist right so it wouldn't come out in a huge dribble. "You like pasta? What, which pasta? Making different doughs, different shapes, stuffed pasta, what?"

"Yeah," said Jude. When she stared at him, he added, "All of it. I made… I made a lot of stuffed pastas. Made a list of all the, uh, the… shapes. Ticking 'em off as I work through 'em, and different doughs, too."

Vanessa smiled, and he felt like trying to sprint out of the place, but unfortunately, his fucking leg was broken.

"What are you doing after this course is finished?"

He shrugged. "They say another month, maybe two, for my leg. Then PT."

She was still looking at him. "And after that?"

"Sail."

"You're a sailor?"

"Deckhand."

"If I got you a trainee job, would you take it? For now, for the next few months?"

Jude turned to stare at her.

"He's a chef, and he's always looking for a good galley hand," said Vanessa. "He's working as a private chef right now, and he's going back to chartering once his kids are back to school full time, but he always wants a good second. A guy like you is right up his street."

Jude didn't say anything, felt like there was a spotlight being shone directly into his face.

"Yes?" she asked. "No?"

"My leg," said Jude.

"You couldn't join a crew right now anyway," said Vanessa, "but he'd pay for you to help him do big events for now, feel out your skills — and you get around in here okay."

"Now?" Jude asked.

"I'll call him," said Vanessa. "He's been asking me to keep an eye out, someone without too much ego — he likes for his kitchen to be easy-going, and you're easy-going, right?"

Jude didn't say anything, and didn't nod his head, because he fucking *wasn't* easy-going.

"Okay," said Vanessa, with a grin. "Pasta, huh?"

"Yeah," said Jude.

At the end of the day, Rich got out of the car to take the box of cakes off him before Jude could even make his way down the ramp, and Jude pulled him closer by the front of his shirt, into a kiss.

Rich let out a pleased sound, cupping the back of his neck and leaning into it, and Jude's cheeks were burning, his heart pounding hard in his chest, but it felt good. Natural. Nice.

"Hope you didn't think you could distract me from this," he murmured against Jude's mouth as he lifted the box away from where Jude had been balancing it in the crook of his arm, and Jude laughed.

"Nah, it's all yours," he muttered. "Take my satchel too?"

"Sure. A *kiss*. Where people can see — in public!"

"Fuck off," said Jude, putting his hands back against the crutch handles and continuing down the ramp as Rich cracked open the box, took out one of the cakes, and bit into it.

"Mmm!" he exclaimed.

"Molten centre," said Jude. "Real fucking dick-twist."

Rich chewed around cake, crumbs lingering on his lips, and swallowed. "I think dick-twists are good, if this is the result," he said. "More penile rotations for Saint Jude. I'll write that down."

"Eat your fucking cake, Rich."

"Gladly!"

Once they were in the car, Jude said, "Tutor wants to get me a job."

"As a cook?"

"Galley hand."

"You can't sail with a broken leg, even in the galley."

"She said he's working as a private chef until school term starts up. That he's looking to train someone before then."

"That sounds good," said Rich, but his tone was gentle. "Do you want to do that?"

"Don't know. Said yes."

"You might not like it," said Rich reasonably. "But you might really enjoy it."

"The fuck does a galley hand even do?" asked Jude, trying to think if they'd ever had one. "Cook for crew?"

"Cook for crew, cover chef's holidays. Organisation of the kitchen inventory — you'd liaise with stews, obviously, and the chef. Cleaning the kitchen, washing dishes, keeping everything organised. That you already have your STCWs and your basic courses under your belt would likely be a point in your favour."

Jude was silent for a few moments, looking out of the window.

"I like cleaning," he said. "I don't like stuff being dirty, but it doesn't bother me, cleaning stuff up."

Rich smiled, reaching across to pat his knee, and didn't say anything.

* * *

Rich got his certificate framed, and asked Sam to put it up behind the bar in the Marlin. Jude came in and everyone started laughing even before Rich came up behind him and shoved a costume chef's hat onto his head, and then Jude started laughing too.

It was embarrassing, made his cheeks burn with heat — he hated too much attention, had never been able to cope with it, but as much as it made him feel like he was about to explode, they were all nice, and people kept clapping him on the shoulder.

People didn't really ask about his dad when they saw him anymore — they asked about Rich, sometimes, but mostly, they asked about Jude. How his leg was healing up; how his cooking classes were going; if he'd managed to get himself sent to the hospital again yet.

Like he was real, like he was... a person, just, on his own.

It was weird, but not bad, exactly.

"Now you've tried both," Rich murmured hot in his ear hours later, "do you think you prefer topping or bottoming?"

"Not sure," Jude said vaguely, so blissed out he could barely move, Rich rubbing idle circles on his back. "More data needed. Gotta experiment."

Rich laughed at him.

"Don't laugh! What's your favourite food I've cooked?"

"Oh, *definitely* more data needed," said Rich firmly, pressing kisses into the small of his back and tracing the line of his spine up between his shoulders. "Gotta do more research."

* * *

That Monday morning, he cooked pasta, just a simple fresh tagliatelle tossed with prawns and mussels, and brought it down the hill and into the harbourmaster's office. Rich was chewing out a guy for not passing some kind of fire safety inspection on his boat.

It was hot, seeing Rich all stern and angry.

He never got like that with Jude, even mockingly — Jude was pretty sure if Rich came at him like that he'd either start throwing punches or throw up on Rich's shoes — but it was interesting to see, *different*, attractive.

It was controlled. It wasn't like when Jude got angry, didn't involve him hitting things or people. He kept it close into himself, like he was about to explode, and although he never raised his voice above a certain level, never shouted, the guy flinched at his cold tones as if he was screaming.

"Hi, Jude," said Rich when the guy had walked off, tail between his legs. "Felt like a walk?"

Jude put the Tupperware box on his desk, and handed him a fork.

Rich grabbed his hand and kissed the back of it, making a loud, dramatic smack of his lips, and Jude groaned.

"What is it? No, don't tell me. It'll surprise me. You sensed I was pissed off enough to forget lunch?"

"I guess I must have. I'm gonna go meet that chef now."

"Am I meant to save some of this for him?"

"Nah, it's all yours."

"Good, I would never have given any up. Have fun. Good luck?"

Jude nodded. "Can you, um... Not now. But could you show me how you paint models?"

He'd watched him to do it a little. Watched him prime the little plastic figures and then get out tiny little brushes with long sticks and paint all the details on top, layering the colours.

"You want to try it?" asked Rich.

"I think I could make moulds," said Jude. "Not — Not right now. Not for a while. But I was thinking I could copy some of your figurines, um, and you can make custom moulds for chocolate? And then I could... paint them. But as cake decorations. For your, um, birthday, or — Because you like them. It's not a surprise, sorry. But not just you, I could, um, Maria's son likes soccer, so I was thinking I could practice making his soccer team and painting their, uh, their uniforms. But..."

Rich was staring at him, his mouth open, and he slowly stood to his feet.

Jude swallowed, anxious, but Rich put his hands on Jude's cheeks, held him like he was cupping the whole of Jude's life between his palms, and kissed him.

"Yeah," he said, his voice slightly hoarse. "Yeah, that sounds... Really nice, Jude. I'd be happy to show you."

"I upset you?"

"I'm not upset. I may be misty-eyed like a man beset with longing in an Austen novel, but *upset* is not the word."

"The fuck does that mean?"

"It means you're wonderful," said Rich, and kissed him again.

Jude felt like crawling into the ground, felt like his skin might just burn off he was so hot, and he mumbled, "I gotta go."

Rich nodded, cupping his cheek again.

Jude wanted to say something else, wanted to say something... good. Nothing came out when he opened his mouth.

* * *

He expected to meet a stressed-out yacht chef ready to shout at him: there was a high turnover of chefs on his dad's boat, and that was the archetype he'd come to expect from them.

Instead of an angry little guy, though, the guy waiting was broad-shouldered and solid, with tattoos banding his shoulders and his thighs in complex patterns, and he did not seem to be super stressed, or stressed at all. He had a very firm handshake, and he looked at Jude critically, thoughtfully.

"Vanessa said you had a broken leg."

"Yeah."

"Gonna take long to heal?"

"Two months more at most," said Jude. "It was a clean break, but it fully came apart and they had to set it back in place in surgery, so the whole bone has to knit back together, not just a fracture."

"Physical therapy after, huh?"

"Yeah."

"You have PT before?"

"Sure."

"Broke bones?"

"Strained my shoulder."

"When?"

"I was twenty."

"You play rugby?"

"Uh, a little."

"I like rugby. You?"

"It's fine."

"You don't talk much."

Jude hesitated, trying to think of the right thing to say, not sure what the right answer was, but the chef looked pleased, giving a slow nod of his head.

"My name's Teo. Vanessa tell you I'm a private chef right now?"

"Yeah."

"I normally do the huge charters, the big boats, so I like a second guy in my galley."

"Makes sense."

"You got formal training?"

"From Vanessa."

"You cook much before that?"

"No."

"Huh," said Teo, smiling and nodding his head. "Vanessa sent you my way, so you must be good."

"I don't know."

Teo smiled wider. "Come prep with me," he said.

Teo corrected the way he held a knife, and made him swap over when he used the wrong one; he showed him how to chop faster, told him about the different coloured chopping boards you used to make sure you didn't cross-contaminate raw fish with raw meat with vegetables with cooked meat. It made sense, segmenting them out.

Teo was forty-four years old, he was Samoan, he liked rugby, and he had two daughters and one son.

It didn't seem to bother him that Jude wasn't great at small talk, or at talking much at all — if anything, he seemed delighted that Jude took instruction.

When he asked how Jude felt about washing dishes, and Jude said he found washing dishes relaxing, he clapped his hands together and laughed.

"You're fucking *perfect*," he said, and it didn't actually sound like sarcasm.

"Thanks," Jude said.

Teo's wife was named Niki: she also liked rugby. She was a doctor, a GP, and she did a lot of work with yachties and tourists. Jude wondered if Rich knew her, knew Teo.

Rich knew everyone.

"You married?" asked Teo. "Engaged?"

"No," said Jude. "You…" He hesitated, but it was the first time he'd started a real sentence without prompting, and Teo was looking at him raptly. "You know, um, you know Richard Chastain?"

"Baptiste Chastain's boy, the harbourmaster? Of course I do."

Jude nodded stoutly. "Mm."

This was evidently not the clear statement of romantic attachment Jude had hoped it would be, because Teo stared at him in bafflement for a good ten seconds before he said, "Oh, you mean you're dating him?"

"Mm," Jude grunted again.

"You like a wild man, huh?"

"He paints toy figures," said Jude. "For people who play with trains. If he's a wild anything, it's a wild nerd."

Teo had a great laugh, one that came from the very base of his belly, and it echoed around the kitchen.

After a moment or two of hesitation, Jude smiled back at him.

* * *

Teo kept him on, over the next few weeks, and Jude liked it.

Teo was working as a private chef at the moment, but he normally worked on big yachts, and he liked to cook big meals.

"I like complicated flavours," he told Jude, "but that doesn't always mean a hundred moving parts, huh? It means balancing everything. Sometimes you can make more complexity with five ingredients than you could with fifty."

Jude liked to watch what Teo did, copy him — sometimes, it seemed like stage magic, the stuff he did with his hands, folding pastries or cutting pieces of meat, his hands moving so fast that what they created seemed like it had been pulled from thin air, but he'd slow down when Jude wanted to do as he was, until Jude could watch him, really watch him, and all the steps suddenly made sense.

He told Jude what must have been a hundred stories about his family — his kids and his wife, his brothers, his aunts and uncles, his grandparents, his *great* grandparents, his ancestors.

He was very connected with stuff like that — and he talked a lot in general, said a lot, connected everything that to Jude never really seemed connected.

Jude liked that.

"We tell stories with food," said Teo. "We remember the food we ate on different occasions — tastes, smells, textures, appearances, they all connect to memories, put us in contact with everyone who cooked this way before us, all our family, all the innovators. Food lets us share culture, community, family, friendship — it's art, it's science, it's craft, it's *love*."

"Yeah," agreed Jude.

"You don't talk much," said Teo. "Just like to appreciate things, huh?"

Jude was quiet for a little while, kneading bread dough, and forced himself to say, "It's... hard."

"Talking?" asked Teo, raising his eyebrows.

"Yeah. I... I'm trying."

"You think it'll get easier? You'll talk more the more you know me?"

"I guess," said Jude, kneading dough.

"You play hard to get," said Teo mock-seriously, and Jude chuckled.

"I'm like... I'm like dough," he said. "I need— Time. Work. To warm up, to build, um, structure, with someone. But then I'm— Then I'm better. I think."

Teo's smile was full and genuine, and to Jude's surprise, he didn't feel excruciatingly humiliated, or like he wanted to die. He felt... Normal. Well, maybe not normal. But he felt okay.

"What's your family like?"

"I have two brothers," said Jude. "James and Jonah."

"Triple-J!"

"My father is Captain Corey James Jupp."

Teo's smile froze a little, but it didn't go away completely. He was still gentle when he talked to Jude, but it occurred to Jude that everyone knew Rich's dad and always said good things about him, always talked about him like he was great, like he was amazing, like he was... good.

Most people didn't really react to mentions of Jude's dad like that. In the Hamptons, around Long Island, people were always impressed by his family, but that was different to personally liking his dad, thinking he was actually a good guy.

"Tough guy on the island," said Teo.

"Yeah," said Jude. "I'm not really... like my father."

"Nah," agreed Teo, and then smacked him playfully on the arm and started talking about his son's pet tarantula, which terrified him, but he'd been trying not to let that on to the kids.

They made pasta.

* * *

His dad and his brothers came back a few weeks later.

His father was cold and brimming with anger when they came home to Jude in the kitchen, with Rich sitting at the dining table sipping wine.

Jude saw his brothers move to take their bags upstairs.

"You shouldn't be on that leg," said his father from the kitchen doorway.

"I'm not on it," said Jude. "No weight on it, anyway. I'm making lobster tails, then rib-eyes. Rich said Guy quit and walked off the boat when you guys made port, so I figured you'd be hungry."

"Captain Jupp," said Rich pleasantly. "Would you care for some wine? I brought two bottles over with me — it's a very full-bodied merlot."

"Are you going to be joining us for dinner, *Mr* Chastain?" asked his father, pronouncing the *Mr* like it was an insult.

"Yeah," said Jude. "He is."

"Can I talk to you for a moment?" asked his father.

"Sure, I'm listening," said Jude. He didn't move. When his father tapped his foot impatiently, he said, "I'm doing the first fry on these potatoes and mixing the garlic butter. It'll take me five to get the lobster in the oven to broil."

"Then, Chastain, leave me alone with my son."

Rich didn't move, staring Jude's dad down, and Jude felt his lips twitch.

"It's okay," he said quietly, and Rich stood to his feet. He poured Jude's dad a glass of wine and handed it to him as he passed, but his father immediately put it down again.

"The rumours I'm hearing true?" asked his father.

"Which ones?"

"The rumours about you."

"Which ones?"

"You and *Chastain*."

Jude met his father's gaze. "Which ones?"

"Word has it on the island that you've been walking around arm-in-arm with him, all fucking dewy-eyed," said his father sharply, voice rising. Jude watched the butter, garlic, and herbs bubble and shift as he whisked the mixture in the bowl held under his arm. He listened to the regular hiss of the whisk wire against the metal surface. "Is that it? Past thirty and you decide to become a gay chef?"

"I'm no good at being a straight deckhand," said Jude. "You don't even think so."

He heard his father inhale sharply, and he didn't turn to look at him as he lifted the bowl up, drizzling butter over each lobster.

"That's not true," said his father.

"Yeah, it is. I'm bad at it. Being a deckhand. Too slow, not good at jumping into shit, bad at rigging, not into watersports."

"And it's taken you thirty years to fucking decide that?"

"No," said Jude. "Just a few months away from you, I guess."

He couldn't quite believe that he'd said it when it came out of his mouth, and he looked at the butter as it sank in around the lobster flesh on each of the five tails. He picked up the tray, slotting them into the oven, and then he took the fries out of the fire and shook out the basket, patting the fries dry with kitchen paper.

"You can't just decide to throw away your whole life at your age," said his father.

"I don't think I am," said Jude. "Don't have much of a life to throw away."

"Oh, you don't think? Everything I've done for you, Jude, years of raising you, training you, *teaching* you, all thrown away so you can bake cakes and play with seafood!" His volume was getting louder and louder. It was hurting Jude's ears, but Jude didn't say anything, wiping off his hands with a cloth, and his father went on, "You've always just been too fucking shy, and if you'd just get over it and—"

"It's not about you," he said quietly. "I'm not doing this against you, to hurt you. I'm doing it for me."

"Not doing it against me," said his father sharply, with a loud, sarcastic laugh, slamming his hand down against the window sill. Jude flinched at the loud clap of it, but his father's fist wasn't anywhere near his face. "I'm your *father*, Jude. You're rejecting everything I've ever taught you boys — how is that not *against* me?"

"Am I your least favourite son?"

His father stared at him, looking horrified, so Jude stopped looking at his face and set the egg-timer.

The dial was shaped like a lobster. Rich bought him six of them with different sea animals. Jude held it in his hand, felt it tick.

"No," said his father.

"Maybe you'll like me better, like this," said Jude. "I do."

"So you decide to be gay all of a sudden, and it's a coincidence you take up with someone who is constantly at odds with me and my work, who works to undermine my reputation? You don't think that your sudden *conversion* might have something to do with him?"

Jude wondered if Rich could hear this, with how loudly his dad was shouting. He said, "I don't think I decided all of a sudden. I think I just... never let myself think about it."

"Well," said his father. "Suddenly you're a cook, you don't want to sail, you want to fuck a man, a man who hates me — that isn't sudden?"

Jude didn't want to keep arguing about it. He didn't want to talk about it at all. He picked up the glass of wine and put it back in his father's hand, and said, "This'll take about ten more minutes."

His father, to his surprise, actually went into the dining room.

It looked official, formal, his father and his brothers still in their whites, and Rich wearing a tight sweater over his shirt, a neat one that looked expensive.

When his father wasn't looking, Rich made a kissy face at Jude through the open kitchen door.

Jude gave him the finger, and Rich laughed.

Dinner went well.

"This is *great*, man," said James when they were eating the lobster, and Jonah groaned over the rib-eye, kept reaching over to slap Jude on the back as they were eating.

Rich, mercifully, kept his moans to a minimum, but Jude could see he was enjoying it.

"You working with Teo Elisala?" asked James.

"Yeah," said Jude. "Just casually. He's a good chef — he's maybe looking for a galley hand in the fall. Depending on how my PT goes, he'd like to take me on."

"So not even a chef's position?" asked his father. "Washing pots and pans?"

"'Stead of windows and decks?" asked Jude.

James held his breath, Jonah freezing beside him, and his father set his jaw.

"The salad is wonderful," said Rich, unbothered. "I love the vinaigrette."

"Thanks."

"Is there dessert?"

"No."

"He's so cagey," said Rich to the others. "Keeps his courses a secret."

"Maybe I don't want you to go rummaging in the fridge for anything before it's time."

"Ah, so there's something in the fridge? Would you gentlemen excuse me for a moment?"

Jude laughed as Rich pretended to get up, although he was nervous, but then his brothers laughed too, and that was—

That was a relief.

Dessert was a chocolate teacup filled with mousse and a really light sponge — the chocolate was fucking murder to temper, dipping glass bottoms in the chocolate and trying to get it to cool evenly.

His and Rich's were undeniably the ugliest, and Jude's especially didn't have the nice shiny finish the chocolate was meant to.

Rich put the plates out for everybody, and Jude followed behind, pouring cream and raspberry sauce hot from the hob until it filled the cups to their brims, soaking into the sponge inside.

"Beautiful," Rich whispered in his ear, and they sat down to eat.

"Is this your recipe?" his father asked.

"Uh, yeah, the sponge is lemon and raspberry, I've been working on it a little. The sauce is mine too — the cup is just tempered chocolate."

"... You made the cups?"

Jonah had lifted his up to drink the sauce from the bottom, and James had broken his into pieces with his spoon, but both of them had turned to stare at him now.

"Yeah," said Jude, feeling that uncomfortable under-the-spotlight anxiety again. "I used the round water glasses with the heavy base, dipped them in molten chocolate, and then flipped them upside down to chill.

The handles are just thick chocolate, I poured the shapes between two sheets of plastic, and then I held the edges to a hot pan to melt them a bit before attaching them to the cup. The chocolate is its own glue."

"I thought you must have bought them," his father said quietly, picking up the cup by its handle, swilling around the contents inside. Jude felt like dancing when he said, at length, "It looks good, Jude."

He took a bite of the cup.

Jude grinned.

"Is that *it*?" demanded Rich at the end of the night, when Jude was sitting in his passenger seat and they were driving back to his. "The teacup is *good*? Not I love you! Not I love your work! Not I support you, or I'm sorry, or fucking anything, just — Just, *It looks good?*"

"Both hands on the wheel, babe."

"My hands are on the wheel," Rich grumbled.

He'd been ranting for a little while, and Jude was surprised by how relaxed it made him feel, for Rich to say all that, to be on his side, and be on his side so unflinchingly.

He couldn't stop smiling. His face ached from it.

"For him, that's good," said Jude. "And he didn't keep shouting at me, or throw a punch, or... or ask weird questions. Or pick a fight. For him, that was big."

"Captain Prick," muttered Rich, undeterred.

"Thanks," said Jude. "For coming."

"I'll go wherever you ask me," said Rich, and Jude felt dizzy from smiling.

"Would you still want to date me?" asked Jude. "If I, if I take the job with Teo, if he wants me? If I go to sea for weeks, months at a time?"

"I'd starve while you were gone," said Rich. "Absence makes the heart grow hungrier — and my cock, too."

Jude laughed so hard he couldn't stop.

"You can't cook?"

"Sure, I can a little. Not like you can."

"Guess I'd have to freeze meals for you, then," murmured Jude. "Keep you happy."

"You make me happy," said Rich.

Jude wanted to say it back, wanted to echo the sentiment, but he didn't feel like he could, exactly, his mouth feeling full, his tongue empty.

"Yeah," he said finally.

Rich was smiling. Rich knew what he meant.

FIN.

More from the Author

If you'd like to seek out more of my work, *Heart of Stone* is a full-length novel set in the 18th century, and is a slowburn slice-of-life romance between a vampire and his secretary, the vampire ADHD and the secretary autistic. It has a lot of humour and domestic elements throughout.

My most recent release, *Powder and Feathers*, is a long-form contemporary dark romance with a great many fantasy elements, featuring a fucked-up dynamic between a Fallen angel and a depressed artist he begins stalking in the park.

If you're interested in perusing more novella-length pieces and short stories, I publish a huge variety of short stories that are available on a subscription model from Patreon[1] or as part of your Medium[2] subscription!

I normally publish at least one new piece a week, whether that's short stories, longer form short stories like this one, serial updates for my chaptered works, or non-fiction pieces like essays and analyses.

My name is Johannes T. Evans on both sites.

My website: www.JohannesTEvans.com[3]

My Twitter: @JohannesTEvans[4]

And finally, if you'd like to get regular email updates from me, with media recommendations, links to my most recently published work, and other little announcements, you <u>can sign up at www.buttondown.email/ JohannesTEvans.</u>

---

1. https://www.patreon.com/JohannesEvans

2. https://johannestevans.medium.com/directory-of-work-6291c6e102b9

3. http://www.JohannesTEvans.com

4. https://twitter.com/johannestevans

Also by Johannes T. Evans

Lashton Town
Gellert's New Job
Daddy's Boy
A King's Man
King's Sentence

Standalone
Heart of Stone
In Perpetuity
Scattered Stories (Short Story Compilation)
The Mermaid and the Fisherman
Divine Service
Gerald Poole and the Pirates
Powder and Feathers
Cold Comfort
More Than Coffee
Touch-Starved
Divine Bodies
Fallen Dust
Hunger at Sea
The Angel in the Woods
Archival Management

The Widower's Garden
Au Naturale
The Lord of the Wood's Spring Bride
Agony and Ecstasy
Sleeping Beauty
Sweet On
A Gift for the Wolfmen
The Stasis Box
Saint Jude's Kitchen
Alexander's Angel
Ambitious Men
Remnants of a Bygone Era
Dirk and the Weaver
Unlikely Matches
Like A Thief and an Assassin
Deep Breath
Good Coin
Agreements and Curses
Bone-Eater, Hungry for Fire
The Devil's Mark
The Many Deaths of Baldr the Undying
For Want of Time
Room for Dessert
Paper Houses
Steps Ahead
Hitting the Books
Workplace Connections

9 798227 532763